AF228525

PORTLAND TIMBERS

BY SAM MOUSSAVI

SportsZone

An Imprint of Abdo Publishing
abdobooks.com

abdobooks.com

Published by Abdo Publishing, a division of ABDO, PO Box 398166, Minneapolis, Minnesota 55439. Copyright © 2022 by Abdo Consulting Group, Inc. International copyrights reserved in all countries. No part of this book may be reproduced in any form without written permission from the publisher. SportsZone™ is a trademark and logo of Abdo Publishing.

Printed in the United States of America, North Mankato, Minnesota
052021
092021

Cover Photo: Kamil Krzaczynski/AP Images
Interior Photos: Tom Hauck/Getty Images Sport/Getty Images, 5; Rick Bowmer/AP Images, 6–7, 19; Ringo H. W. Chiu/AP Images, 9; David Blair/Cal Sport Media/AP Images, 11; Paul Vernon/AP Images, 12; Robert Houston/AP Images, 15; Greg Wahl-Stevens/AP Images, 17; Darryl Dyck/The Canadian Press/AP Images, 20; Ted S. Warren/AP Images, 22, 37, 40; Brent Wojahn/The Oregonian/AP Images, 24; Don Ryan/AP Images, 26; Rick Egan/ The Salt Lake Tribune/AP Images, 29; Chris Brown/Cal Sport Media/AP Images, 30; Brian Murphy/Icon Sportswire, 33; Larry C. Lawson/Cal Sport Media/AP Images, 35; Diego Diaz/ Icon Sportswire/AP Images, 39, 43

Editor: Patrick Donnelly
Series Designer: Dan Peluso

Library of Congress Control Number: 2019954427

Publisher's Cataloging-in-Publication Data

Names: Moussavi, Sam, author.
Title: Portland Timbers / by Sam Moussavi
Description: Minneapolis, Minnesota : Abdo Publishing, 2022 | Series: Inside MLS | Includes online resources and index.
Identifiers: ISBN 9781532192616 (lib. bdg.) | ISBN 9781644945698 (pbk.) | ISBN 9781098210519 (ebook)
Subjects: LCSH: Portland Timbers (Soccer team)--Juvenile literature. | Soccer teams-- Juvenile literature. | Professional sports franchises--Juvenile literature. | Sports Teams--Juvenile literature.
Classification: DDC 796.334--dc23

TABLE OF CONTENTS

ROSE CITY
BREAKTHROUGH

The Portland Timbers missed the Major League Soccer (MLS) playoffs in 2014, and there was little reason to believe 2015 would be any different. Portland began the 2015 season with its two best players, midfielders Diego Valeri and Will Johnson, sidelined by injuries suffered the season before. The loss of Valeri was especially difficult. He was a brilliant attacking midfielder and one of the Timbers' best players at setting up and scoring goals.

With much of the team's offensive production on the sidelines, Portland tied in its first three regular-season games. Then the Timbers lost their fourth game to rival Vancouver. It wasn't until their fifth game, against FC Dallas, that they finally broke through with a win. But that did not

Portland's supporters' group, the Timbers Army, celebrates a goal in 2012.

put an end to the team's uneven play. The Timbers notched victories in just three of their first 12 matches.

Eventually, though, the offense found its footing. The team rattled off six wins in its next seven matches. Portland was finally able to put together strong offense with a stingy defense. In the six victories, the Timbers averaged two goals per contest. That was an improvement from their first 12 games, when they averaged less than half of that. The team also allowed only two goals combined in the six wins.

Fanendo Adi celebrates his penalty kick goal against Real Salt Lake.

Although they were winning, the margin of error for the Timbers was slim.

That proved to be a problem when inconsistency struck again. The main issue was that Portland simply could not put together a complete match. Injuries were a problem too. The absence of key players contributed to a rough patch beginning with a 3–0 loss at Philadelphia on July 11. The Timbers went on to win only three of their next 11 matches. That left Portland in danger of missing the postseason again with only three games to go.

STANDING TALL

The stakes were high in a late-season match at Real Salt Lake. Forward Fanendo Adi scored on a penalty kick early in the second half, and Portland squeaked out a 1–0 win to keep its slim playoff hopes alive. The Timbers next visited the defending MLS champion, the LA Galaxy. This time Portland erased a 1–0 halftime deficit by exploding for five goals in the last 25 minutes of the match to win 5–2.

That made it two straight victories in must-win games. Portland's playoff hopes rested on the final regular-season match against the Colorado Rapids. It was simple. With a win, Portland would qualify for the postseason. A loss would send the Timbers home for the winter.

The Timbers started fast against Colorado. After just two minutes had passed, Adi headed a ball off the top of the goal frame. Adi's near miss set an aggressive tone for the Timbers, though. Just three minutes later, midfielder Darlington Nagbe nailed a free kick from just outside the penalty area to make it 1–0 Portland. But the match would not be easy. Colorado scored an equalizing goal in the 13th minute. If the Timbers wanted the playoffs, they would have to earn it.

Darlington Nagbe played a big role in the Timbers' late-season surge to the playoffs.

Nagbe struck again in the 33rd minute when he headed a perfect cross into the back of the net. Portland took the lead 2–1 and didn't look back. The Timbers added two more goals in the second half to seal a 4–1 victory and a playoff berth. Portland solidified its playoff seed, finishing third in the Western Conference. The win against Colorado was important

for another reason. It meant Portland would host its first
playoff match against Sporting Kansas City four days later.

PLAYOFF TIME

Portland faced off with Sporting KC in the knockout stage of
the MLS Western Conference playoffs. The knockout stage
is a winner-take-all game—the winning team moves on and
the losing team goes home. The teams played to 2–2 tie after
120 minutes of play. That meant they had to settle the match
by penalty shootout.

After five rounds the teams were tied at three. From there,
the shootout went to sudden death—one round at a time
until one team was ahead. But the two sides matched each
other in each of the next four rounds. To start the 10th round,
Portland goalkeeper Adam Kwarasey stepped up to shoot.
He banged home the goal to give the Timbers a 7–6 lead in
the shootout. If Kwarasey could stop KC's next attempt, the
Timbers would win. And that's just what he did. Kwarasey came
up with a double-fisted, diving save to seal the victory. It took
a complete team effort, but Portland defeated Sporting KC to
advance. The Timbers' improbable run continued.

Next up for the Timbers was Vancouver in the conference
semifinals. This round was set up in an aggregate format.

Portland's Liam Ridgewell (24) celebrates his goal in the first leg of the Timbers' playoff victory over FC Dallas.

The team with the most goals after two matches, or "legs," would win the series. The first leg in Portland was played to a 0–0 draw. But the Timbers won the second leg in Vancouver 2–0. Portland won the series 2–0 on aggregate—or total goals—and moved into the Western Conference finals.

The Timbers faced conference champion FC Dallas. This round of the playoffs had the same aggregate format. Portland stormed to a 3–1 win at home in the first leg. The second leg in Dallas was played to a 2–2 draw, giving the Timbers a 5–3

Diego Valeri scored in the first minute of the MLS Cup to put the Timbers ahead to stay.

victory on aggregate. After an entire season of uneven play, Portland was now one win away from winning the MLS Cup.

The championship match pitted Portland against the Columbus Crew in Columbus. The Crew finished second in the Eastern Conference and had knocked off the first-place New York Red Bulls in the conference finals. But the Timbers would not be intimidated. Valeri struck 27 seconds into the match to put Portland on top. The goal was the fastest score in MLS Cup history. Winger Rodney Wallace doubled the lead for the Timbers just six minutes later.

Columbus got on the board in the 18th minute, cutting the Portland lead to 2–1. The Timbers had plenty of chances to score again during the rest of the match but could not. However, Portland's defense was up to the task. They shut down the Columbus attack for the rest of time. Valeri was named the match's Most Valuable Player (MVP) after his early-game heroics. The 2–1 victory gave the city of Portland its first major professional sports title since 1977. The scrappy Timbers were not perfect. But between Valeri's creativity and Adi's marksmanship, Portland's offense caught fire at the right time.

The Timbers were on top of the American soccer world with their improbable run to the Cup. But that was not always the case. The team rose from humble roots to reach the heights of the soccer world in 2015.

PACIFIC NORTHWEST
REIGN

Pro soccer existed in the city of Portland long before the MLS Timbers were born. The present-day Timbers are considered a continuation of the Portland franchise that started in 1975. Those Timbers played in the North American Soccer League (NASL).

The 1975 Timbers squad was successful right away. The team made it all the way to the NASL's championship game, which was called the Soccer Bowl. Portland lost in the 1975 final, but the season was not a waste. That amazing first season proved that fans in Oregon could support a professional soccer team. The Timbers benefited from the faith and loyalty of a passionate fan base. Portland earned the nickname "Soccer City, USA."

Chris Dangerfield (13) makes a play for the Timbers in the 1975 Soccer Bowl.

FACING TWO LEGENDS

During the 1977 NASL season, Portland squared off against two of the most famous players in the world. One was Franz Beckenbauer, captain of West Germany's 1974 World Cup champions. Another was Brazilian superstar Pelé. On August 28, 1977, both Beckenbauer and Pelé suited up for the New York Cosmos against the Timbers. The final match of Pelé's pro career took place later that year when Portland hosted the Soccer Bowl between the Cosmos and the Seattle Sounders.

The original Timbers made the NASL playoffs three times. The franchise folded in 1982 due to financial issues, and the league followed soon after. Three years later, a new independent club calling itself FC Portland was formed. In 1989 the club was acquired by local businessman Art Dixon, who changed its name to the Portland Timbers. Dixon put a lot of money and care into the return of his beloved Timbers. Like so many other proud Portlanders, Dixon had been a huge fan of the NASL Timbers teams.

Once again the Timbers experienced rapid success in a new league. They finished their first season in the Western Soccer League (WSL) with a record of 11–5. The team made it to the Northern Division semifinals. The instant success provided even more evidence that pro soccer belonged in Oregon.

Portland went on to play in various second-tier pro soccer leagues, including the United Soccer League (USL)

Brian Winters (11) and the Timbers faced major league competition from the San Jose Earthquakes in the 2004 US Open Cup.

First Division. The Timbers fared well in those leagues, making the playoffs seven times in 10 seasons. In 2004 and 2009, Portland earned the USL First Division Commissioner's Cup. That was a trophy given to the team with the best regular-season record. The 2009 season was particularly memorable as the Timbers went on a 24-game unbeaten streak. That was not only a USL record but one of the longest undefeated streaks in US professional soccer history.

MAKING THE JUMP

Following all of the Timbers' success in the second division, the city of Portland was granted an MLS franchise in the spring of 2009. The team would retain the name "Timbers" as its nickname. One hurdle needed to be cleared in order to begin play, however. The city's existing stadiums had numerous problems with seating and the field. MLS officials wanted the Timbers to have a stadium designed specifically for soccer. Eventually the Timbers' ownership decided it was best to renovate the existing PGE Park, a minor league baseball stadium, rather than build a brand-new stadium. The renovations were finished in 2011, and Providence Park—as it was later renamed—opened in time for the start of the MLS season.

The Timbers' new home was a refurbished minor league baseball stadium that opened in 2011 when they joined MLS.

John Spencer was the MLS Timbers' first head coach. The team struggled under Spencer, winning only 16 of 51 games before he was fired midway through his second season. But 2012 wasn't completely devoid of success.

One of the benefits of the Timbers joining MLS was that it renewed the Portland-Seattle rivalry. The cities are natural

Timbers players celebrate winning the Cascadia Cup after a 1–0 victory over Vancouver in 2012.

foes in a lot of ways. Timbers and Sounders teams had faced off since the 1970s in the NASL. The rivalry continued with the minor league versions of the teams as well. The series ended when Seattle moved up to MLS in 2009, but it resumed when the Timbers joined them in 2011. And for good measure, another longtime foe, the Vancouver Whitecaps, joined MLS that year too. The three teams battle each year for the Cascadia Cup, named after the Cascade Mountain range.

While all of the Cascadia Cup games are heated, Portland and Seattle matches have a special fire. Seattle came into MLS with bright-colored uniforms and played in front of huge crowds in a high-tech, modern football stadium. The Timbers have maintained a more organic feel that better reflects their city. All of this comes together to create electric atmospheres whenever the teams meet.

Portland won the Cascadia Cup as an MLS team for the first time in 2012. But some of the Timbers' most memorable meetings with the Sounders were still to come.

A NEW ERA BEGINS

The year 2013 marked a milestone for the franchise. The Timbers hired new coach Caleb Porter. He led the team to a first-place finish in the Western Conference. The Timbers caught fire early, going on a 15-game unbeaten streak, and they never looked back. The banner season clinched Portland's first MLS playoff berth.

Timbers keeper Jeff Attinella makes a save against Seattle's Raúl Ruidíaz in Portland's thrilling playoff victory in 2018.

The Timbers contended for the title again in 2018. But not without the inconsistency that had hurt the team before. Portland once again qualified for the playoffs late in the season. With a win in the knockout stage against FC Dallas, the Timbers had a date with Seattle in the conference semis. The series against their Pacific Northwest rivals proved to be one for the ages.

After two matches, the Timbers and Sounders were tied 4–4 on aggregate. But Portland advanced with a 4–2 shootout victory. Then the Timbers defeated Sporting KC on aggregate. They finally came up short in the MLS Cup, losing to Atlanta United 2–0. The Timbers' flair for the dramatic has been a consistent part of the team's MLS legacy. Another has been the team's star players showing up again and again.

TIMBERS
TO REMEMBER

New head coach Caleb Porter changed the franchise in 2013. Porter had significant coaching experience before coming to the Rose City. He had coached the US Under-23 men's team as well as the men's team at the University of Akron. In fact, Porter led Akron to the national championship in 2010. Porter's track record of winning made him the ideal coach for the Timbers. Just 38 years old at the time he was hired, Porter could relate to the team's youthful roster while also commanding respect with his résumé.

Porter led the Timbers to immediate success. The team won 14 games and lost only five in 2013. Portland finished with 57 points, the best mark in the Western Conference.

Caleb Porter had no MLS coaching experience when he took over as the Timbers' head coach in 2013.

Diego Valeri, *right*, brought creativity and toughness to the Timbers lineup.

Those 57 points remained a franchise high through 2020. The exceptional run helped Porter win MLS Coach of the Year.

Porter's peak with the Timbers came in 2015. He led the franchise to its first MLS Cup win. Porter coached the Timbers for five seasons before leaving the team in 2017. His teams made the MLS playoffs three times, and his 68 wins remain the most in Timbers history.

DIEGO ARRIVES

Expectations were high when midfielder Diego Valeri arrived in Portland in 2013. The Argentina native lived up to the hype right away—and then some. In his Timbers debut, Valeri scored one goal and set up another. Valeri is a creative player who can attack a defense from any spot on the field. He is known for setting up teammates with his craftiness in tight spaces. He has been a main offensive piece since joining Portland on loan from Argentina's Club Atlético Lanús in January 2013. He won MLS Newcomer of the Year in 2013. Valeri also earned his first of three MLS Best XI appearances during the team's breakout 2013 season.

Valeri also set several MLS records during a magical 2017. He broke the league record for most goals by a midfielder with 21. He became only the second midfielder in MLS history with at least 20 goals and 10 assists in a single season. Valeri also became one of only 18 players in MLS history to reach both 50 career goals and assists. He was named the MLS MVP that season. In his first eight seasons with the Timbers, Valeri scored

84 goals and had at least a share of the team scoring lead five times. He also was an MLS All-Star four times.

One player who has helped Valeri thrive is another Diego—Diego Chará. The Colombia national arrived in Portland in 2011. Though perhaps not as exciting as Valeri, Chará has proven to be similarly vital. The 5-foot-8 midfielder plays a defensive role, breaking up attacks before they can get into a dangerous position. Chará has proven to be one of the league's most effective tacklers.

A third South American player, Sebastián Blanco, joined them in 2017. The Argentina native was a natural attacking player, notching 26 goals and 35 assists in his first four seasons.

CAPTAIN WILL

Canadian midfielder Will Johnson was known as a versatile player during his time in Portland. So likable was Johnson that

Diego Chará (21) quickly became a mainstay in the Portland midfield.

he was named a captain by Porter less than a year after joining the Timbers.

Johnson was a steady player on Portland's 2015 championship team, but his best individual season came

Darlington Nagbe appeared in more than 200 matches in seven seasons with the Timbers before leaving for Atlanta United in 2018.

in 2013. He scored a career-high nine goals and earned a spot on the MLS Best XI. Johnson also made the 2013 MLS All-Star team. Johnson played 69 games in three seasons with Portland

and was named the Timbers Supporters' Player of the Year in 2013.

OUT OF AFRICA

The Timbers have had plenty of success with players from African nations. One was Liberian center back Darlington Nagbe, who played with Portland from 2011 to 2017. Nagbe was selected second overall in the 2011 MLS SuperDraft after a stellar college career at Akron. His first goal with Portland was a jaw-dropping volley from the top of the penalty area. The spectacular scoring strike earned Nagbe MLS Goal of the Year in 2011.

Nagbe's best season came in 2013 after reuniting with Porter, his college coach. He scored a career-high nine goals. He also won the MLS Fair Play Award. That award is given after each season to the player who best represents sportsmanship on the field. Nagbe earned another Fair Play Award as well as an MLS All-Star nod in 2016.

Nigerian forward Fanendo Adi joined the Timbers in 2014. He arrived on loan from Danish power FC Copenhagen. After four goals in his first few matches for Portland, Adi earned a permanent spot. He was a mainstay from 2014 to 2018. Adi scored 54 goals during his time in the Rose City, second only to Valeri. With a goal against the rival Seattle Sounders in June 2017, Adi became the first Timber to score 50 goals for the franchise.

TIMBERS ARMY

Some of the most important people in Timbers history have never set foot on the field. Timbers Army was founded in 2002, when the team played in the USL. The supporters' group has lived on ever since, following the club through its journey to MLS. Timbers Army is known as one of the loudest and most raucous fan bases in US soccer. The group is famous for its green and white scarves and deafening chants. You can also hear the faithful members of Timbers Army banging massive drums during matches.

The Army gathers at the North End of Providence Park for each home match. The extraordinary support comes in part from the rich soccer history in Portland. Though most MLS franchises have supporters' clubs, few are as passionate about their team as the Timbers Army.

Timbers Army members use drums to set the tone for the match.

CHAPTER 4

TIMBERS
MOMENTS

With constant fan support in the stands, the Timbers blossomed quickly upon joining MLS. The 2013 MLS season was a key point in the development of the Timbers. The first big move was Timbers' ownership bringing in new coach Caleb Porter. On the day he was hired, Porter promised that the team would not back down to anyone. Porter also promised at his introduction that his team was "here to win games and trophies."

Porter's words proved to be true as Timbers fans saw a hard-nosed team from the start of that season. Although the team did not win until its fifth game, the first four matches were close and hotly contested. Porter's Timbers were fast

Goalkeeper Donovan Ricketts played a huge role in Portland's strong 2013 season.

and physical. They relied on defense to keep the ship afloat until the offense caught up.

One of the main reasons for the strong defense that year was Jamaican goalkeeper Donovan Ricketts. On his way to the MLS Goalkeeper of the Year award, Ricketts made acrobatic saves seemingly every match. His sprawling stops kept the Timbers in nearly every game. Ricketts made 92 saves in 32 starts. He stopped 74.8 percent of the shots he faced in 2013. That was the second-best mark among all MLS goalkeepers.

By the end of the season, Portland's offense was firing on all cylinders as well. The Timbers' attack was led by Diego Valeri, Darlington Nagbe, Diego Chará, and Will Johnson. All four players set personal records in the Timbers' banner season. A dynamic offense and a stingy defense made Portland a tough matchup for their opponents heading into the 2013 playoffs.

On the way to a franchise-high 57 points, the Timbers dominated the Western Conference. The team lost only five matches during the entire regular season. Another strength of the 2013 team was its ability to avoid long losing streaks. Portland had only one two-game losing streak the entire season.

Will Johnson celebrates a goal against Seattle in the Timbers' 2013 playoff victory.

The Timbers' crowning moment in 2013 came in the conference semis against Pacific Northwest rival Seattle. They defeated Seattle on aggregate, including a thrilling win in front of their home fans in leg two. The series victory moved Portland into the conference finals in just their third season in MLS. And though the dream of a championship ended against Real Salt Lake, the foundation for a winning culture had been set in 2013.

ANOTHER PLAYOFF RUN

The 2018 season brought back memories of the team's magical run at the end of 2015. Once again Portland was up and down during the regular season. The Timbers started out slow before going on a six-game winning streak. They fought through a four-game losing streak late in the season, only to find their footing in time to make a playoff run. As he had before, Valeri propelled Portland's offense with 10 goals. Sebastián Blanco also spurred on the Timbers' offense, tying his countryman, Valeri, with 10 goals.

New coach Giovanni Savarese pushed the right buttons as he guided the Timbers to 15 wins and a playoff appearance. Portland faced FC Dallas on the road in the knockout stage. Valeri scored twice to give the Timbers a 2–1 win.

Timbers coach Giovanni Savarese calls out instructions during a 2018 match.

The win set up a date with the Seattle Sounders. Seattle was one of the league's most dangerous teams, having reached the previous two MLS Cups as well as winning in 2016.

Dairon Asprilla (27) and keeper Jeff Attinella are mobbed by their teammates after they combined to defeat Seattle in a playoff shootout in 2018.

The Sounders had also won that year's Cascadia Cup. But the Timbers had won two of their three regular-season matches against the Sounders, setting up a tense playoff series.

The first leg of the semifinal was played in front of Timbers Army at Providence Park. Seattle struck first, scoring a goal in the 10th minute. But Portland did not panic. Jeremy Ebobisse tied the score in the 17th minute. Blanco scored again in the 29th minute, giving the Timbers a lead they would not surrender. Portland took the first leg 2–1.

In the second leg in front of a frenzied crowd in Seattle, the Sounders led 3–2 after extra time. That left the rivals tied 4–4 on aggregate. This meant a penalty shootout would determine who would move on to face Sporting KC in the conference finals.

Portland goalie Jeff Attinella came up huge in the shootout. The American stopper blocked two Seattle attempts, and the Timbers' scorers did the rest. Once again it was Valeri and Blanco who came up huge. The two Argentines converted their kicks before Colombian forward Dairon Asprilla sealed the win for Portland. The Timbers took the series against their Pacific Northwest rivals and moved on to face Sporting KC.

GOING ALL THE WAY?

The Western Conference finals opened with a scoreless draw in Portland. That meant the second leg in Kansas City would determine who would advance to the MLS Cup. The match

Construction to Providence Park forced the Timbers to play their first 12 games of 2019 on the road. By the time they returned home, they were just 4–6–2. But Portland battled back. The Timbers closed out the 2019 season with points in their final four games. That included a 3–1 win over San Jose in the season finale that clinched sixth place in the Western Conference. However, Portland's season ended in the first round of the playoffs at Real Salt Lake.

reached the 90th minute tied 2–2, which was an advantage to the Timbers. Because they had scored two away goals, they would advance by a tiebreaker. But before the game could head to extra time, the official added nine minutes of stoppage time to the end of the second half.

That gave Sporting KC an extended opportunity to take the lead. Instead, the Timbers defense held on, and Valeri added an insurance goal in the final seconds as Portland reached its second MLS Cup.

Unfortunately for the Timbers, their thrilling ride came to a disappointing end. Atlanta United, hosting the MLS Cup in just its second year in the league, scored once in each half and cruised to a 2–0 victory. Still, the steely backbone showed by Timbers players gave fans hope for more trophies in the near future. And with return trips to the playoffs in 2019 and 2020, the Timbers indeed showed

Forward Jeremy Ebobisse tied for the team lead in goals in both 2019 and 2020.

they were still a force to be reckoned with in MLS' tough

Western Conference.

TIMELINE

1975	2009	2011	2011	2012
The Portland Timbers are born in the NASL.	MLS announces the Portland Timbers will be reborn as an MLS expansion team.	The Timbers play their first MLS regular-season match, a 3–1 loss at Colorado on March 19.	The Timbers jump out to a 3–0 lead and hang on to beat Chicago 4–2 for their first MLS victory on April 14.	Caleb Porter is named the Timbers head coach on August 29.

TEAM FACTS

FIRST SEASON

2011

STADIUM

Providence Park (2011–)

MLS CUP TITLES

2015

KEY PLAYERS

Fanendo Adi (2014–18)
Sebastián Blanco (2017–)
Diego Chará (2011–)
Jeremy Ebobisse (2017–)
Jack Jewsbury (2011–16)
Will Johnson (2013–15)
Adam Kwarasey (2015–16)
Darlington Nagbe (2011–17)
Donovan Ricketts (2012–14)
Maximiliano Urruti (2013–15)
Diego Valeri (2013–)

KEY COACHES

Caleb Porter (2013–17)
Giovanni Savarese (2018–)

MLS MOST VALUABLE PLAYER

Diego Valeri (2017)

MLS NEWCOMER OF THE YEAR

Diego Valeri (2013)

MLS GOALKEEPER OF THE YEAR

Donovan Ricketts (2013)

MLS COMEBACK PLAYER OF THE YEAR

Rodney Wallace (2014)

MLS COACH OF THE YEAR

Caleb Porter (2013)

MLS FAIR PLAY AWARD

Darlington Nagbe (2013, 2015)

GLOSSARY

aggregate
The combined score of both games in a two-legged tie.

extra time
Two 15-minute periods added to a game if the score is tied at the end of regulation.

goalkeeper
A player whose primary duty is to prevent the ball from entering the net.

loan
An agreement to allow a player to play for another team for a single season or less.

midfielder
A player who stays mostly in the middle third of the field and links the defenders with the forwards.

penalty shootout
A tiebreaking shootout after stoppage time to decide who wins a game.

rival
An opponent with whom a player or team has a fierce and ongoing competition.

sportsmanship
Fair and generous behavior or treatment of others in a sports contest.

stoppage time
Also known as added time, a number of minutes tacked onto the end of a half for stoppages that occurred during play from injuries, free kicks, and goals.

supporter
A fan of a soccer club.

versatile
Able to adapt or be adapted to many different functions.

volley
A ball that is kicked out of the air rather than from off the ground.

MORE INFORMATION

BOOKS

Kortemeier, Todd. *Total Soccer*. Minneapolis, MN: Abdo Publishing, 2017.

Marthaler, Jon. *Ultimate Soccer Road Trip*. Minneapolis, MN: Abdo Publishing, 2019.

Trusdell, Brian. *Soccer Record Breakers*. Minneapolis, MN: Abdo Publishing, 2016.

ONLINE RESOURCES

To learn more about the Portland Timbers, please visit **abdobooklinks.com** or scan this QR code. These links are routinely monitored and updated to provide the most current information available.

INDEX

ABOUT THE AUTHOR

Sam Moussavi is a novelist and freelance writer based in the San Francisco Bay Area. He has written two sets of young adult novels as well as many nonfiction sports titles.